MariJo Moore

red woman
with
backward eyes
and other stories

RED WOMAN WITH BACKWARD EYES

AND

OTHER STORIES

MariJo Moore

rENEGADE
pLANETS
pUBLISHING

An American Indian Owned Company

Printed on Recycled Paper

Also by MariJo Moore

Spirit Voices of Bones

Crow Quotes

Tree Quotes

Desert Quotes

Feeding The Ancient Fires: A Collection of Writings by North Carolina American Indians (editor)

Website: marijomoore.com

First Edition August 2001
Edited by Beth Carter of mamabird. com
Author photo Beth Carter ©2001
Inside art Darrin Bark ©2001
Layout and cover design by Phil Olson of Fishlips Creative

Library of Congress Catalog Card Number: 2001-132101
ISBN # 0-9654921-7-6

rENEGADE pLANETS pUBLISHING
P.O. Box 2493
Candler, NC 28715
phone: 878-665-7630 • Fax: 828-670-6347 • email renegadepl@aol.com

for my son

Stephen Lance Jaynes

in memory of

Dustan Paul Moore, Cornelius Hansford Moore,
Pearl Anna Thurmond Moore, Ruby Macklin Love, and
Fanny Florence Cornelia Ellen Childers Love

CONTENTS

ACKNOWLEDGMENTS

The author offers deep felt gratitude to the following people:

Beth Carter for excellent editing and complete understanding of the necessity of creativity.

Kathryn Cooper, Vicki Plemmons, Barbara Braveboy–Locklear, and Dr. Susan Gardner for endearing encouragement.

Vine Deloria, Jr., Kimberly Roppolo, *Studies in American Indian Literatures*, and Dr. Lee Francis for selfless giving of time and reviews.

Darrin Bark and Phil Olson for brilliant artistic additions.

Marie Love, Frances King, Joseph L. Moore, and my brothers and sisters for love and emotional support.

Special thanks to Dr. Joan Elliott and Mrs. Theda Mount for encouraging me to follow my dream of writing.

To the following publications in which versions of some of these stories have appeared:

Racing Home: A Collection of Stories by NC Award Winning Authors
The Paper Journey Press: "Siren's Voices"

Voices From Home: The North Carolina Prose Anthology
Avisson Press, Inc. : "Rumors"

Blue Ridge Peaks: "The Colored Mountain"

SPIRIT SONGS: A Contemporary Native American Fabulist Anthology
Invisible Cities Press: "Red Woman With Backward Eyes"

Mother Tongue : "Suda Cornsilk's Gathering"

Wild Mountain Times : "Howanetta and the Eyes of the Dead"
("Sacrifices")

INTRODUCTION

There is a type of loneliness that infects one's soul. A loneliness that tears a hole that can never be sewn back together. No matter what color the thread. No matter how sharp the needle. No matter how many attempts are made to weave the torn soul with another's, the tear remains. This is the loneliness I have felt most of my life.

Being of mixed-race is not easy. It never has been and I suppose it never will. I am not dark enough for some and not light enough for others. Because I was not raised on a reservation, some say I don't belong to the Indian race. Because I have Indian blood, some say I don't belong to the Caucasian race. For years I wrote "Other" beside the box requiring race specification.

Cherokees have intermingled their blood with non-Indians for centuries. When my great, great paternal grandparents were married in 1824, a Cherokee Nation census listed 73 non-Indian women married to Cherokee men, and 147 non-Indian men married to Cherokee women. A friend once remarked, "If anyone tries to blot out the mixed-bloods, John Ross and Sequoyah would have to be blotted out as well as many others."

For a while, I tried repairing the tear in my mixed-race soul with alcohol, relationships and other diversions. But nothing worked. Nothing. The tear was to become a creative outlet, the birthplace of my writings. Sharing these writings evinces my refusal to have any part of me ignored, canceled, or blotted out.

Taking into consideration the modern, traditional and ancestral stories my Cherokee grandaddy, Irish grandmothers, and Dutch/Cherokee grandaddy and great grandmother had told me, I began to accept their stories as medicine – sometimes strong in the healing, sometimes gentle. These stories became an integral part of my spiritual growth. By remembering them, I could accept my place as one who lives in two worlds. I could stop treating myself as a victim and accept my total self.

As I began interlacing the stories of my grandparents with my own experiences, anxious spirits of those who had passed to the other realm began visiting my dreams, urging me to voice their revelations through my writings. By sharing their stories of how alcohol, drugs, self denial, hate, anger, fear or misunderstandings could lead to destruction of one's soul, the spirits were giving warning to others dealing with the same issues.

The stories in this collection are a webbing of dreams, spiritual intuition, personal experiences and ancestral memories. Some may make you laugh, others will make you cry. Some tell of the survival of torn, infected souls who do not give up, regardless of the circumstances. Some tell of judgment's strangling grip tearing the hole of loneliness even wider. Some of the stories have no earthly explanation.

The names of all characters were fabricated; the Tennessee and North Carolina settings are real.

MariJo Moore
Candler, North Carolina
April 2001

"At my age, and with so much mixing of bloodlines, I am no longer certain where I come from," said Delaura. "Or who I am."

"No one knows in these kingdoms," said Abrenuncio. "And I believe it will be centuries before they find out."

Gabriel García Márquez

Of Love and Other Demons

RED WOMAN WITH BACKWARD EYES

RED WOMAN WITH BACKWARD EYES

Every day the girl sits, facing North beside the pond to which her mama gave herself. I watch the girl staring across the stillness as if expecting her mama to rise from her watery death, sit beside her on the overgrown bank and smooth the girl's dark hair with fingers of silk. Today, as every day, I send the black snakes to sit beside the girl, providing wise company during her wait. Three of them, coiled, shiny and content, semicircle her – one to her right, one to her left, and one just in front. They wait with her. Every day. "She will come," the snakes tell the girl. "She will come."

After two hours, often times three, just before the dampening twilight arrives, I tell the snakes to uncoil. They stretch, raise their crystal heads into the cooling darkness and move off in different directions. I watch the girl as she leaves the pond bank, leaves her waiting, and goes to the house of her grandmother, Mama Mamie.

Mama Mamie shares her home with the girl and her identical twin great aunts. The two great aunts have not always lived here. They came after the girl's mama gave herself to the refuge of the pond water, and they stay all the time now.

As I watch the girl walk toward the tiny clapboard house, I hear her thoughts. She thinks of how she hates the confinement of school. She knows how to read and write; her mama taught her when she was five. Now, she is seven and doesn't want to be taught by anyone else.

Dust rain has forgotten covers her toes as she begins to run. The too-tight blouse she has long outgrown hugs her brown body. Her well-deep eyes reflect the feeling of disappointment in her heart of not seeing her mama today. She misses her terribly. "You will see her soon," I whisper into the girl's ear.

I sit atop the slanting roof and observe what goes on inside the little house. This is my duty. I am to watch over this child until it is her time to come with me. It won't be long.

"She's been sittin' on that pond bank again," Lottie or Lucille says. The girl doesn't care to tell them apart. "I can smell it on her! I can smell the scum."

The girl smells her blouse but smells nothing but the dusty breath of the black snakes. Scum does not smell dusty.

"Leave that child be!" Mama Mamie is standing over the stove, back hunched into the movement of her left hand stirring a pot of fish stew.

"I guess she thinks her mama's just gonna come back," Lottie or Lucille says. "I guess she thinks her mama's just gonna pop up out of that water, all clean and good and alive as ever!" she exclaims, clapping her hands together at the words "pop up."

The girl ignores her aunts and hovers close to her grandmother. Mama Mamie takes a cold, hard biscuit from her apron's pocket and gives it to the girl. She goes into the adjoining living room and sits in front of the two televisions stacked atop each other. Lottie and Lucille slouch on the sinking floral couch and watch the tiny people flicker across the screen of the bottom television and listen to the sound of their voices drifting from the smaller one on top.

"Whew, it's hot in this kitchen," Mama Mamie complains but no one listens. Lottie or Lucille says, "I guess she's just dumb. I guess the girl is just dumb as a bucket of rocks." The girl turns slightly to look at the great aunt who has spoken. She sees the black snake I have sent crawling up the twin's fat legs to her fatter thighs. The two identical women stare at the girl. She turns her attention back to the two televisions.

"Don't you remember we buried your mama over two months ago?" The great aunt without the snake speaks. "Do you want me to take you over to the cemetery and show you just where they put her drowned body? Her self-drowned body? I can show you the marker that says 'Sara Ela Hawini. Born July 20, 1972. Died August 27, 1996.' Come on, I'll show you right now."

The great aunt with the snake crawling up her legs begins to snicker but stops abruptly when Mama Mamie slams her wooden stirring spoon on the kitchen table. The snake drops noiselessly to the floor and quickly crawls through a hole in the wall, leaving a trail of ashes. The girl can see it slither toward the pond, on its way to join the two snakes resting near a weeping willow streaked black by lightning.

"You two think I don't know why you came here to live? You two think I think you came here to help me out with that child?" Mama Mamie points the stirring spoon toward the back of the girl's head. A storm gray cat jumps from a cabinet top to lick the stew spillings falling from the spoon to the floor. A half butter bean escapes the bottom of the spoon and wedges itself into a hole torn in the fading linoleum rug. The cat scratches quietly trying to free it. "Better you go into my gut than theirs," the girl hears the cat say to the half butter bean.

The girl doesn't like to look at her twin great aunts but she is intrigued by their similarities. Their wrinkles are the same. Even the fat on their arms hangs the same. They puff on their Vantage Menthols the same, trying to stick their overweight tongues into the tiny holes in the ends.

The girl focuses on the cat. I leave the roof and sit in the rocker on the front porch. I whistle and rock but only the girl hears me.

"You two think I don't know you've lost everything you had to that damn gambling mess they've built over there?" Mama Mamie says, jerking the stirring spoon toward the front door. The cat watches with quiet fascination, hoping for another half butter bean. "I know all about it! *ALL* about it! And the rest of the family knows as well!"

The aunts do not answer. They turn back to the televisions and their heated soap "stories."

Mama Mamie lays down the stirring spoon, unties her apron, slings it across the back of a cracked blue vinyl chair leaning against the table and says, "Supper's ready. I'm going outside to cool off." She motions for the girl to follow her.

The cat goes with them, rubs his body against the girl's legs for a moment, then pounces off after a butterfly. "I like things with butter in their names," the girl hears the cat say.

I watch the girl and Mama Mamie as they make their way down the path that winds through the cornfields bivouacking the little house. The wind rattles through the bent husks and reminds the girl of me. It is the same clattering noise made by my necklace of bird bones. The first sound the girl heard when I began visiting her on the pond bank several weeks ago. She has taken note of my red skin and white eyes locked backward, but she has asked nothing. She knows me as Red Woman With Backward Eyes.

"Your mama didn't die of suffocation. She didn't die of drowning," I told her. "The Nunnehi knew your mama was dead long before she walked into the haven of that water," I explained as I pointed my long, spindly fingers toward the muddy pond. The snakes around her quivered with flooding vibrations made by unwatered truth.

"Her heart became stagnant and stopped beating a long time ago – even before you were born. The only problem was she didn't know it had stopped beating. She imagined it but didn't know it. Not for sure." I told the girl these things and she believed me. My words swirl in her thoughts often. She has come to understand I am here for her.

Mama Mamie is worried about the girl. She thinks the girl

spends too much time alone since the death of her mama. "Tell me, Ama, doesn't it make you sad to sit next to that pond everyday?" Mama Mamie looks deeply into the girl's wind moistened eyes trying to pull her attention into the present. The girl turns around to see if I am still behind them, but I have shifted to sit atop a rusted tractor resting in the dying cornfield.

"Tell her about Red Woman With Backward Eyes!" a fat, insipid raven screams with the authority of a woman giving birth. "Tell her!"

"Mama Mamie, who are the Nunnehi? The Spirit People? Is my mama with them now?" the girl asks.

A maniacal gust of wind shakes the torn husks, scattering brown silken memories long thought forgotten. Harder and harder the wind blows. So hard all the clouds are blown into the next county. So hard sparkling dust from low hanging stars begins to settle on the dead husks. The wind blows the girl's unanswered dreams into the plowed soggy field next to the pond. I catch them and bring them back to her heart. The girl begins to wonder if she has angered the Nunnehi by asking about us. She looks around and shudders.

"No," I whisper so only she can hear. "No, you haven't angered us."

Mama Mamie looks at the girl with deep questioning in her old woman eyes. She decides it is time the girl begins to understand. "Yes, your mama is with the Nunnehi now. And I suppose that's the way she wanted it for quite some time. You're here with me, though, and that's what matters." She brushes the girl's streaming hair with her pained, curved hand and turns to walk back to her kitchen – her sanctuary. The girl notices her grandmother is walking slower than usual. Her heart begins to hurt.

I join the girl on the pond bank the next afternoon. "Eyes, that's what she first saw of your daddy. It was his eyes," I tell her.

"Your mama wasn't worth a hoot after she saw those strange liquid amber-colored eyes of his."

"Was he Indian?" She doesn't look at me though I know she wants to.

"Course he was. She wouldn't have had it any other way, you know that." The bird bones around my neck clatter incessantly above the sleeping snakes. The girl listens to my words as if she were suffocating and they were air. I am Red Woman With Backward Eyes. The girl knows I speak with authority.

"Where did she meet him?" The girl pretends she is not scared of me, but her small hands are shaking.

"She met him in her dreams. Then in her soul. Then in her bed. He told her things only spoken in bed. And then you were conceived. Now, go and tend to your grandmother. She longs to see your young face."

As the girl heads back home, seven silent crows follow above her. I need to do my work, to make preparations. "The girl is almost ready," I tell her mama. "Almost ready."

It is four days before I see the girl again. She has gathered courage from the seven silent crows that carefully circle Mama Mamie's house. The girl thirsts for more answers.

The snakes around her dream quietly as she waits patiently on the bank, calling me with her pondering mind. Hearing a clatter, she knows I have come. At once I am sitting beside her.

"I have some more questions." The girl speaks deliberately, without emotion.

"I'll tell you what you want to know. The time is ripe," I say. I feel the girl watching my scarred hands fingering the bird bone necklace circling my taunt, withering neck.

"Why are your eyes backward like that?" she asks.

"So I can see into the past, into the future, and into now. When I was a young girl, I was taken away from my home, from

24

my family. Put in a place where they tried to take all the Indianness out of me. The people there made me get on my knees, clasp my hands, look up into their heavens, and pray to a god I didn't know and could no way understand. I asked my beliefs that my eyes be rolled backward so those who were making me pray their way would leave me alone. My eyes stuck. No one bothered me after that."

Satisfied with my answer, the girl asks another question. "Was my daddy one of the Nunnehi when my mama met him?"

Suddenly, a silence dense as thick fog envelops us. The left snake moves as if to inhale the stillness. A coldness falls around the girl's shoulders. She shivers, inducing more coldness.

"There," I tell her. "There is your daddy. Feel him? He wants to take you to see your mama. Are you ready to go?"

Fear grips the girl's heart. A fear she has never experienced. Fear made from an equal mixture of excitement and foreboding.

"Do you hear that drum? That thundering in the distance?" I point toward the West where the warm, sweet corn sun is dripping into a basket of mountains. "It is the call of the Nunnehi. Listen to it. Let it cleanse the fear polluting your heart. Listen."

I watch the girl as she listens with her ears. She cannot hear the drumming. She closes her eyes and listens deeply.

"Yes," she whispers. "I can hear the drumming. I want to see my mama!" Tears roll down her soft brown cheeks like shiny rain droplets.

"So, then you shall."

The girl allows me, Red Woman With Backward Eyes, to take her hand and lead her into the pond riddled with answers. Her last thought as she feels the cold, muddy water seeping into her nose is of Mama Mamie.

"She'll be OK," the girl hears her mama's delicate voice assuring her. "You can help me watch over her now."

The pond closes slowly over the top of the girl's head as the three black snakes spin across the water, erasing any ripples. The drumming rolls deeper into the smudged sky and stops.

I have done what I have been called to do.

A screech owl flies from the top of the calm, breathtaking water and disappears into the approaching enormous night.

notes:
Ama: Water
Ela: Earth, ground
Hawini: Deep
Nunnehi: The Spirit People

SIREN'S VOICES

SIREN'S VOICES

Siren could hear voices. At the age of seven she heard the voice of one of the Old Ones whisper in her ear, "Go and tell your mama to stop messing around with that judge." Siren knew it was the voice of one of the Old Ones because of the smell that circled the voice. It was the smell of the aged. The voice smelled just like the faded photographs her Aunt Mandalynn kept in a tattered cigar box underneath her bed.

Siren hid underneath this bed whenever her Aunt Mandalynn and Uncle Jeb fought, and they fought quite a bit around Jeb's pay day. She and her mother had left the mountains of East Tennessee and gone to live with her mother's older sister in the western part of the state when Siren was just a baby. Her daddy had died in a hunting accident (more like a drunken brawl she had heard her mama say several times), and so her young mother was left to fend for herself and her baby. The tiny turquoise house belonged to her Aunt Mandalynn, the cramped living situation adding to the aggravation of the family.

"Who is this woman right here? The one holding the baby?" Siren asked one Saturday afternoon after a loud screaming match between her aunt and uncle. Jeb had slammed the screen door behind him proclaiming, as usual, that it would be a cold day in hell before his shadow would darken the inside of this crazy house again.

"He'll be back when he gets horny," Siren heard her Aunt Mandalynn mutter underneath her breath. She was standing at the sink in their skinny kitchen, peeling potatoes and whistling something that sounded like "When The Saints Go Marching In."

Mandalynn had had the great fortune of attending Mardi Gras down in New Orleans when she was a teenager. All that saintly music had etched a furrow in her brain in which no other type of music could ever grow, no matter what she tried to plant there. No matter if she listened to Pat Boone singing "Love Letters in The Sand " fifty times a day, she still woke up with the sound of Fats Domino singing "I'm Walking To New Orleans" coming from her whistle box as she liked to call it.

"I said, Aunt Mandalynn, who is this?"

"Now where did you get that?" Mandalynn's voice rose to the ceiling and bounced back atop Siren's head.

"I found it."

"Found it where?" Mandalynn's eyes narrowed and reminded Siren of a snake she had seen in a Tarzan movie the week before.

"Found it out in the yard, laying right next to that old John Deere tractor sitting next to the barn." Siren not only heard voices, she also lied a lot.

"That's one of the.n old pictures I keep underneath my bed, now ain't it? What are you doing under there? Look at you! Dust balls all in your hair! That's your old granny's granny and you should have more respect than to go messing around in other people's things. Go put it back! Now!"

"She talked to me this morning." Siren said this matter-of-factly, just as she would have said "It's stopped raining."

Her aunt stopped peeling and looked her dead in the eyes. "What do you mean, she talked to you this morning?"

"I knew it was one of the Old Ones talking to me because the voice smelled just like all those old photographs underneath your bed. So I just had to see which one it was, and I'm pretty sure it was this one. What's her name? She's Indian like us, ain't she?"

"You never mind what's her name or what she is! And you quit lying, you sharped-tongued, nosy youngun! You march your little butt right back in there and put it right back where you found it! I'll tell your mama when she gets home and she'll whip your little butt for real!"

This threat didn't scare Siren because she knew it would be late when her mama got home. She was out with the judge and they had probably gone over to St. Louis or somewhere where they thought no one would recognize them. Like no one would pay any attention to a fat old balding judge and a beautiful raven-haired young woman hugging and kissing on each other. And besides, whenever her mama came home late, she slept most of the next day, and more than likely Aunt Mandalynn would have forgotten about the entire incident by then.

The voice of one of the Old Ones whispered once more as Siren pulled the tattered cigar box from beneath the bed, "Be sure and tell your mama to stop messing around with that judge."

When Siren told her mama what the voice of the one of the Old Ones had whispered in her ear, her mama eyed her suspiciously and then announced in a voice that was heard by the cotton pickers working in the field just down the road, "Well, it's none of your business or anybody else's what I do! And you quit listening to them voices! You hear me? And stop that damn lying!"

But Siren continued to listen to the voices, partly because she liked to listen to them and partly because she didn't like her mama very much.

When Siren was eleven, she found the epic poem "The Odyssey" written by the poet Homer in a library book at school. When she returned home that afternoon, her mama was lying outside in the sun, trying to sweat the beer from the night before out of her system. Siren sat down next to her and began sipping on lemonade her Aunt Mandalynn had left for her in the skinny kitchen.

"Mama, by any chance did you at one time read "The Odyssey" by Homer? You know, the long poem about Odysseus on his way home from the Trojan War? This mythical monster, half woman and half bird, tries to lure his ship full of men over to the rocks where they will crash. Her name was Siren. Is that where you got the idea for my name?" Siren knew she was going out on a limb asking this. She had never seen her mama read anything except *True Confessions* and *TV Guide* occasionally to see if any Clark Gable movies were coming on television the nights the judge couldn't get away from his wife.

"Naw, I never read that," her copper-faced mother said between juicy chews of gum. "I named you Siren 'cause I heard one siren after the other going off the night your daddy made love to me over and over 'till he was sure I was pregnant. There musta been a huge fire or robbery or somethin' somewhere in town 'cause them sirens went off all night long."

Shortly after this revelation, Siren began wearing a white tablecloth over her head when she was at home. When asked why, she would explain in a low, dramatic voice, "Because I don't exist. I am a ghost. The ghost of a noise heard by my mama as she slept with my daddy so many years ago. I am a ghost who doesn't exist."

"Well, for a ghost who don't exist, you sure make one helluva mess," her Aunt Mandalynn said. "Just look at that jelly and peanut butter glopped all over my kitchen chairs!"

"Siren, take that damn thing off your head!" Her mama had tired of this drama after about three days. "Come on, now," her voice softened as she remembered that Judge Ripley was due to come over that evening and she didn't want Siren to embarrass her any more than usual. "Let that beautiful black hair show! You know that black curly hair is the richest thing your daddy could have ever given you."

Siren took the tablecloth off her head. The next day she took her Uncle Jeb's white shoe polish and painted her onyx curls white. When her mama saw this, she made her sit outside in the rain until all the white washed off. "What are them voices saying to you now, Miss Smartie Pants?" her mama asked as Siren came inside, white streaks covering her whole body. "Are they telling you not to be so damned stupid?"

Siren began to tell bigger lies. No one noticed. Siren shaved off one of her eyebrows. No one noticed. Siren cut off her bangs. No one noticed. Siren took a double edged blade from her Uncle Jeb's razor and sliced the inside of her left arm. They noticed.

"I guess them silly ass voices told you to do this, eh?" Uncle Jeb didn't speak much unless he felt like he had something of importance to say or he was watching wrestling on television. He yelled quite a bit then. Sometimes Siren thought the man actually believed all that stuff was real. He had taken Siren to the emergency room at the local hospital where a stringy-looking intern had sewn the flesh of her arm back together.

"Naw, they don't tell me to do bad things to myself. They just tell me things about people. Like for instance, last week, a voice that smelled like popcorn told me that you got several bottles of Jack Daniels stashed out in the barn."

Jeb almost ran the car off the road. "You been watching me?" His upper lip began to sweat. He knew if Mandalynn found out about those bottles she wouldn't let him have any spending money come Saturday night.

"Naw, I got better things to do than follow you around."

"Yeah, like slice away at your arm."

For the next two years, Siren spoke to her family only out of necessity. Mostly she just read, sat in her room, and listened to the voices. Soon she was able to hear conversations between people who were miles away. She also began to read the thoughts of others. After her thirteenth birthday (her mama and the judge gave her a record player and her aunt and uncle gave her a bracelet with ugly charms attached), Siren began taking long walks at night and thinking about how it must feel to be free of thoughts. How wonderful it would be to not have to think- — to not have to listen to the voices telling her things she really didn't want to know. Like how her History teacher, Mr. Walden, was diddling her gym teacher, Miss Nichols. Or about how Harry Jenkins, the town's most prominent banker, was stealing money from his patrons right and left.

When Siren was sixteen, a voice with no odor came to her and said, "Run away from home."

"Tell me, where's your smell?" Siren didn't trust voices with no smell. She was now full of piss and vinegar, as her mama liked to say, and wasn't afraid to talk back to anyone or anything, especially the voices.

"Run away from these crazy people, I tell you, or you'll be sorry."

"Nope. Not 'till you let me smell your smell. I don't listen to voices that don't smell."

"Suit yourself," the odorless voice said.

THE RAIN
by Siren

Thanks for the rain
the beautiful falling silver rain.
Give us a strong storm of consolation
strong beating winds of affirmation
tiny, tiny drops of tantamount receptions
and a pot to piss in.

Rain rain rain down like a son-of-a-bitch
scattering lightning and
scaring us all into asking deeper
questions of our intentions.

Clamoring down
down down
like a whore on a hundred dollar bill
or a baby after a new thought.

At this time in her life, Siren began writing poetry. Some of the writings were her own ideas, but mostly she wrote what the voices told her to write. She liked to think that one of them might be William Faulkner because it always smelled like whiskey and said things like "clamoring down like a whore on a hundred dollar bill."

"Now, she's not only hearing voices, lying a lot, slicing away at herself, but writing nasty poetry too!" her mama screamed when she was snooping through Siren's closet one day looking for a pair of shoes to borrow. "Ya'll come in here and look at this! She's writing nasty poetry!"

"I told you to run away," the odorless voice said.

Three months before her graduation from high school, Siren was watching television and dreaming of the new boy who had just moved to town when she heard someone pull into the driveway. She was home alone and thought it must be a salesman or maybe the Combine Insurance man to collect her Aunt Mandalynn's premium for the month. But when she looked outside, the sheriff's car, looking menacing yet protective, had stopped just three feet from the tiny turquoise house. Sheriff Tom, all six-feet-three-inches of him, came to the front door.

"Where's your aunt and uncle, Missy?"

"They've gone into town shopping. What's wrong?" Siren knew something bad was going to happen because all morning a voice that smelled like a funeral parlor kept whispering in her ear, "She didn't do it. Tell them she didn't do it."

"Well, it seems somebody's done gone and whacked off the

top of Judge Ripley's head. And your mama – now we don't know for sure she did it – but your mama has been arrested for the murder. She's the one who called us to come down to the S&S Motel over on Highway 20. Lord, it was a mess in that room! Looked like somebody been killin' hogs in there."

Siren's sharp tongue climbed to the roof of her mouth and refused to come down. Her mama? Arrested for murdering the judge? Why, she loved that old Coot!

"I reckon it's best you stay here. I'll go and try to find Mandalynn and Jeb and see if they want to get your mama a lawyer. I wouldn't answer the phone or door if I was you. The townsfolk are pretty upset about this whole thing."

He spat tobacco juice into Mandalynn's tulip bed and then left.

Siren's tongue climbed down from the roof of her mouth even before the car had pulled out of the driveway. "What am I going to do?" Where were the voices now that she needed them? "I said, what am I going to do?"

"I told you to run away from home," the odorless voice said. "I told you to tell her to stop messing with that judge," the voice of one of the Old Ones said. "I told you she didn't do it," the funeral parlor voice said.

"Dammit! One of you with some sense come and tell me what to do!" A wisp of Brylcream entered the living room.

"Sit down," the Brylcream voice said. This was a voice of authority. This was a voice she intuitively recognized. This was the voice of her dead daddy.

"Get a piece of paper and write this down. I'll tell you exactly what you are to do."

When Siren's mama went to trial for the murder of Judge Ripley, the whole town was there. Those who couldn't squeeze into the Crockett County courthouse were outside on the steps, screaming things like "Murderer! Adulteress! Shameless Indian Whore Hussy!"

Siren ignored them as she walked into the courtroom and handed the bailiff an envelope. He opened the envelope and read what was scribbled on several sheets of notebook paper. His face turned a bright red. Swallowing hard and trying to regain his composure, he neatly put the pages back inside the envelope and then handed it to the presiding judge who was just entering the courtroom. The presiding judge's face turned a pale shade of green as he read what Siren had written. He then whispered into the bailiff's ear and Siren was brought to the presiding judge's chambers.

"Young lady, where did you get this?" The presiding judge was trying to maintain an air of dignity though his hands were shaking uncontrollably.

"I wrote it."

"Where did you get the information you wrote?" His voice was now shaking as badly as his hands.

"I hear voices. A voice that smelled like Brylcream told me to write those things down and give them to you the day of my mama's trial. That's my mama out there who is being accused of a murder she didn't commit."

The presiding judge looked at the bailiff. "She's got times and dates and places," he whispered loudly. His body was beginning to show stains of sweat through the dark robe.

"I know. I read it," the bailiff answered in an even louder whisper.

"What do you plan to do with this, young lady? You know you could ruin the lives of some very important people in this town." And to the bailiff, "If my wife finds out about us, she'll nail my ass to the wall!" The bailiff shook his head in agreement and looked at Siren with pleading in his eyes.

"I thought I might sell it to you. But if you're not interested, I'm sure somebody down at the newspaper might want to see it."

"How much, I mean, what do you mean, sell it to me?"

"Well, I know and you know that my mama didn't kill Judge Ripley. I know and you know that his crazy, jealous wife is the one that chopped off the top of his head. But I know and you know that you ain't about to arrest her because her family owns half this county. So, I figure if you get my mama off, let her go free, then I'll sell you that information and call it an even trade."

"And you wouldn't tell anyone else?"

"Naw, I'd sign something swearing to that. I know you like to sleep nights, just like everybody else. And I know you wouldn't want everyone knowing just how close you two are." She eyed the bailiff accusingly.

Two weeks later, Siren, her Aunt Mandalynn, Uncle Jeb, and her mama sat in their back yard drinking lemonade. "I'm so grateful to be free of that damn jail!" Her mama spoke between sips of lemonade and drags of Vice Roy. "And I owe it all to my sweet little Siren."

"You never did tell us what you told that presiding judge," her Aunt Mandalynn looked at Siren from behind mirrored sunglasses.

"Naw, and I ain't about to."

Seven months after Siren's mama was released from the murder on a technicality (it seems the arresting policeman had forgotten to read her her rights) she was killed while helping a new boyfriend rob a bank. She stopped breathing as soon as the bullet bit into her heart.

Siren was enjoying a full-paid scholarship, compliments of the presiding judge, at the University of Arizona at Tuscon when she heard the news. "I told you to runaway from home," the odorless voice said. "I told you to tell her to stop messing with that judge," the voice of one of the Old Ones said. "I told you she didn't do it," the funeral parlor voice said. "I told you it would all work out this way," the Brylcream voice said.

"And I told all of you we'd eventually go to Europe with the insurance money, now didn't I?" Siren screamed at them, silencing the voices for at least a little while.

SWEET FACES AMONG SOUR SOULS

SWEET FACES AMONG SOUR SOULS

Several shiny crows sat on separate limbs of a dead oak tree.
Many were screaming and crying, angry with their destinies.
One remained silent except for occasional soft, singing ......

Since there ain't no cedar or sage available, I smudge the stale negative air of the room with my songs, making sweet Cherokee words float in and out of the steel bars confining me. I long ago got to the point where I can't sleep too good. I guess I got nothing pretty left to dream about. So I sing.

They all think I'm crazy in here. Crazy and wild. I feel them staring at me. I know they're listening when I sing my songs, even though they pretend they ain't. They can't understand anyways since they don't know my language. And they don't understand that I *have* to smudge this stinking prison air clean before I can see my grandbabies. And since I ain't likely to get hold of any cedar or sage in here, I smudge with my songs.

There's been a whole lot of pain in my life. It's real hard now to breathe deep without the aching in my heart growing claws and clenching what's left of my few sweet memories. Although it hurts sometimes to remember the sweet, I suck in the cleansed stale air, push it deep into my soul, and allow my grandbabies' faces to surface, collecting at the end of my bunk.

You see, spiritually, I am a strong woman, full of power and full of the mystery. But drinking has tainted the spirit of healing medicine in my Cherokee blood and sometimes I have trouble finding it. Course the bitter memories always come floating into the room, erasing the sweet faces of my grandbabies. After the lights have all been shut out, I lie still in this narrow, hard bunk for a long time, surrounded by the reasons I have to come to know this prison as my home: alcohol and a bad temper. Incorrigible, that's what the judge called me. I didn't even known the meaning of that word until I heard some dyed blonde explaining it the other day.

"It means you can't behave in public worth a damn," she said between choppy chews of Juicy Fruit. "It means you get drunk and show your ass all over the place."

I understood pretty much what she was saying. Is that what I'd done? Had I got drunk and showed my ass all over the place? Too many times.

I drink because I don't know how not to. Alcohol is the curse of my race and has caused no end of heartache to my people. It offers a crooked way out to so many. A way to ease the pains of growing up poor and feeling like second-class citizens. A way to build self-esteem, even if only for a little while. A way to build courage. A way to forget.

You can hear most anything sitting around drinking with the young ones that went off to college and then come back. They said there's two reasons why alcohol has caused so much grief and pain to Indians. One of them said that us Indians couldn't tolerate alcohol because of the sugar in it. For thousands of years before the Europeans landed, we didn't have any processed sugar in our diet and that alcohol turns to pure sugar in the blood, taints it and all. Just like it taints your reasoning. Then someone else said that since us Indians were such spiritual people by nature – being so close to the earth and all – that when evil spirits were put into us by the alcohol, we went absolutely crazy. I don't hardly know which one of these ideas I agree with the most because they both sound pretty convincing to me. I just know drinking has sure caused a world of problems in my life.

It all began with the alcohol I used to smell on my stepdaddy's breath when he came into my room late at night. I guess I couldn't been more than ten. Everything in my life began to be a blur after those times. Even when I was fourteen and a tractor turned over on him and crippled him so bad he left me alone at night, I still couldn't get my mind to function like I wanted it to. I couldn't concentrate in school and didn't want to be close to nobody. I thought something must be really bad wrong with me 'cause of all them things he had done to me. So I began to drink, just like he did.

At first, it had been fun. Drinking beer and running around gave me something to do on boring nights with the other young ones. But by the time I had reached twenty-one, married and given birth to three children, alcohol had become a necessity. An evil friend I couldn't live without, causing much more pain than it could ever relieve.

So I drank and then always wound up in jail, because I am incorrigible. And now I'm in prison. Right here in Raleigh, North Carolina. Seems that judge didn't believe me when I said I wouldn't drink no more. And he sure didn't believe me when I said I didn't mean to slap that woman cop. But she shouldn't been shoving me. It ain't smart to mess with a drunk Indian woman.

I know all these women locked in here with me think I'm crazy. I'm slow and don't speak English too often but I understand it pretty much. And I know my mind ain't all gone. Course the alcohol is going to be the end of me. I know that for a fact. Just like I know that it will cause much heartache in the lives of my grandbabies. I know some of them will have to go through the kind of darkness that comes from swallowing too much of that poison, just like I've had to. But I know some of them will get the message that it ain't no good to drown your soul in man-made spirits.

They're screaming at me again, these locked-up women with their sour souls. I guess they ain't got nothing better to do. As soon as I start my singing, I can feel the air go still, like all of them are afraid of me or something. Then as I get into the spirit of the song and start singing louder, they start screaming at me. They don't like me much, I reckon. Just because I don't talk much and I sing loud and stare into the space at the end of my bunk.

But they don't know this is where I can see the sweet faces of my grandbabies. I see them ever time after I have cleaned this nasty stale prison air with my singing. I don't care if they all think I'm just a crazy Indian woman, I ain't gone so crazy yet that I've forgotten my blood kin. And I can see them, floating there at the end of my bunk. Their dark beautiful faces smiling at their old U ni li si. I can see them plain as day, all seven of them. It's a wonderful blessing to be able to see a collection of sweet faces among all these sour souls.

****

Singing Martha came in this prison wild and full of angry energy, screaming at the top of her lungs, "Dah gwah doh ah Ma di!! Zah lah Gee!" Or somethin' like that. Of course nobody knew what she was screaming because she was screaming in Cherokee. It's a strange language, Cherokee. I've heard some of them speak it over on the Qualla Boundary. Visited there lots of times to go to pow wows and gatherings and such. Even went to a motorcycle rally there once. Some say it sounds like birds chirping when the Indians speak their native tongue, but when they brought Singing Martha in and locked her up two cells down from me, she sounded like a bunch of crazy-ass crows screaming their heads off.

She sings in her cell at night, deep and low, under her breath, but those of us close by can hear her. Then she'll get louder and louder, more and more passionate. Her voice is haunting, scary almost, like an ambulance siren heard late at night. You know what I mean. You hear it, and wonder how close it will come to your house. And then when it leaves your range of hearing, you imagine who might be in it. A woman, beaten up by her old man, a young child, burned on a stove, or someone like me who had gotten strung out on coke and had not known when to quit. Anyways, her voice is like that, interesting and scary at the same time.

I listen to her cry and sing and moan, and somehow it gives me comfort. Not that I think I'm any better off, mind you. Hell, I'm just as locked up as she is. You can't shoot your old man's girlfriend and get away with it now like you could back in the old days. You know, like you see in all them Western movies. A woman back then could blow the crap out of any bitch that might be messing with her old man and the audience would cheer. Most of them anyways. I sure as hell didn't get away with it, so here I sit on my fat ass thinking about it day in and day out and listening to Singing Martha crying and moaning every night.

For about three months now I've been taking classes to get my GED in case I ever do get out on parole. I figure I will, and then I'll need a decent job to support my two kids. Course God only knows what I would do. Maybe get into some kind of management program at Burger King or somewhere. I'd like that. People always said that I had a nice smile. Yeah, I could learn to cook fries and sling burgers, and work my way right into assistant manager in no time.

I know it's strange, but Singing Martha gives me comfort. I think it's because I've been studying poetry in my English class. I like poetry. I like the way it sounds when the teacher reads it out loud to us, and I like the way it feels in my mouth when I read quiet like to myself. I especially like poetry by Emily Dickinson.

Alter? When the hills do.
Falter? When the sun
Question if his glory
Be the perfect one.

Now, that one sounds just like Singing Martha! Hell, she ain't given in an inch since she's been here. Even when the women scream at her to shut up that weird singing, she keeps right on. Like she's calling to somebody or something. Anyways, her singing makes nice background music when I read poetry to myself. I kinda like it. Sometimes I wish I could talk to Singing Martha, tell her how this poetry reminds me of her. But she ain't approachable by no means. She's the type better left alone.

It's been like that for about three weeks now, me reading to myself at night and Singing Martha singing and crying. Then this morning she died. Just up and died right there in her cell. I knew she'd been going through the D.T.'s bad ever since she got here because I'd seen enough of that kind of crap to know what was going on. Shaking and sweating and all that. She needed a drink worsen' anybody I'd ever seen 'cept for my daddy.

Maybe that's what killed her, not having any alcohol. Maybe not having anybody ever come to see her made her die of loneliness. I don't know what goes on in the minds of others. How could I? I still wish I could have gotten to know her. Told her how much her singing meant to me. Maybe even read her a poem or two.

Elysium is as far as to
The very nearest room,
If in that room a friend await
Felicity or doom.

Who am I kidding? She couldn't have understood a word. Or maybe she could. I could have tried, anyways, I guess. I could have tried. But that's the way life goes, I reckon. That's just the way life goes.

It's been quiet as snow falling around here all day since Singing Martha died. At least it was until about twenty minutes ago when I started reading poetry out loud. Now they're all screaming at me like they did at Singing Martha. Guess everybody's got to have something to scream about in here. But I'm ignoring them. I'm ignoring them when they scream, "Shut-up you crazy, poetry reading Bitch!"

I'm ignoring them just like Singing Martha did because now I'm reading for me *and* Singing Martha. And right now I got this crazy feeling she's sitting here on my bunk next to me, listening. Maybe she is. Maybe I'm having flashbacks from all that damn dope I smoked. Who knows? Anyways, I'm reading out loud now and it makes me feel better.

> If I can stop one heart from breaking,
> I shall not live in vain;
> If I can ease one life the aching,
> Or cool one pain;
> Or help one fainting robin
> Unto his nest again,
> I shall not live in vain.

.....And now, all the crows are silent.

note:
U ni li si: Grandmother of a group of children

OLD TSA TSI

OLD TSA TSI

Our Grandmama Toinetta could wring a chicken's neck like nobody's business. We watched, wide-eyed and scared, thinking if she could do that to a chicken, what might she do to us the next time we got into trouble?

Chicken blood would stain her dark hands, drip from her adept fingers, fall through the sticky feathers, and drop to the ground, marking a spot of death. And still we watched. We watched as the chicken became naked but not slick, little stubby places dotting its body.

We watched as Grandmama Toinetta primed the old water pump out behind her house. Primed it with rain water that gathered in a tub just beneath the eaves of the house. The living water breathed life into that old pump, until it burped and gurgled and spat out silver streams that turned red underneath Grandmama Toinetta's dark hands.

We were told that rain water came from heaven. Grandmama Toinetta took us to the Providence Baptist Church every Sunday morning because we were too little to complain and too smart to talk back. It was there we heard a little about heaven and a lot about hell.

Hell. That was where the preacher talked about mostly. We Indian children often wondered if our ancestors who never heard this preacher's rantings and ravings had gone there, but this idea was never discussed.

The preacher said that hell was full of fire and brimstone and bad people who had spent a lot of their time here on earth drinking, cussing, and committing other mortal sins. To us, this place called hell sounded much like a place our Grandmama Toineeta's neighbors would spend a Saturday night, except for the brimstone. We had no idea what brimstone could be. Maybe it was some kind of big rock that people who were going to hell threw at chickens who refused to die from getting their necks wrung. Like our rooster, Old Tsa Tsi. He refused to die.

One early Saturday morning, our Grandmama Toinetta tried and tried to wring that old rooster's neck. We watched and waited. Waited to see his headless body flapping around the side yard, entertaining and scaring us at the same time. But Old Tsa Tsi refused to die. We figured his neck must have been made of rubber or something magical, because it sure wouldn't break in our Grandmama Toineeta's strong, dark hands. She tried and tried and finally gave up. Old Tsa Tsi then walked away proudly as if to say,"The hell with you, Old Woman! It ain't my time to go, and I sure don't want to be sitting on your table at dinner time tomorrow."

After that incident, we weren't scared of watching our Grandmama Toinetta killing chickens any more. We weren't even intrigued. We just accepted it. But we still kept our doubts about the places called heaven and hell, and no one ever explained where all of our ancestors could be.

note:
Tsa Tsi: George

49

MariJo Moore

INDIAN WHEN CONVENIENT

INDIAN WHEN CONVENIENT

I killed my husband this morning.

"She didn't mean to! She didn't mean to! He was a no-good sumbitch, anyway." I hear somebody screaming.

It's one of my sisters, Sara. The quiet one. Damn, I've never heard her be so loud, I think as a cop handcuffs my hands behind me.

The house is a mess. A total mess. "Well, I'll just have to clean it another day," I say to no one in particular, even though there are several people here.

"She didn't mean to. Let her go!" Damn, I wish she would shut up. Hell yes, I meant to. I meant to kill him and I'd do it again if I caught him doing what he was doing this morning. I should have never married the bastard. He was doomed from the moment he was born. I knew it but I've always been a sucker for a loser with dark eyes.

I feel like I know one of these cops from somewhere. Damn, he's a skin. Of course I know him. He used to be married to my cousin, Sheila. What's his name? Bernie, Buddy? Something like that.

My quiet sister is sobbing, almost blubbering. "Please don't take her away." She's grabbing my arms now, trying to pull my hands out of the hand cuffs. I saw a pair of hand cuffs up close one time. Some guy I was having sex with wanted to hook me to the bed and have his way with me.

"Hell, no. I told him. I'm not that drunk or crazy."

I always get the loonies when it comes to men. They seem to be drawn to me. The loonier they are, the more they want to be with me. I guess it's my strength. My opinionated, smart assed self.

I don't know. Maybe it's some sort of karmic thing like the new-agers talk about.

I can hear someone speaking, way far off like. I realize it's the cop I recognize. "Say, didn't you used to be married to Sheila Big Feather?" He ignores me and keeps reading me my rights. "I said, didn't you used to be married to Sheila Big Feather for about fifteen minutes one time?" He looks past me and nods his head.

"Yeah, I thought so. I can see the resemblance in her boy Jason. You ever see him, your son?"

The tag on his shirt reads Sergeant Sims. "Indian When Convenient" is what it should read. He's one of those who thinks he can be white by riding around in a fancy four-wheel drive and marrying a white woman. That's it's OK to fuck an Indian woman, knock her up, marry her for a while, then leave her for a white woman with money.

Indian when convenient. Like during powwows when he wants to show off his light-skinned babies. Or when it comes time to collect his per capita check. Indian when convenient, that's the problem with most Indian men these days.

I guess that one laying over there in his own blood would have been better off if he could have found some rich, white woman. One of those who wants to have Indian babies 'cause one of her granddaddies married some Cherokee woman ten frigging thousand years ago.

"She didn't mean to!" There she goes again.

"God dammit! I DID mean to kill him, Sara. Now shut the fuck up!"

Everyone stops dead still and stares at me. Probably only for a second or two but it feels like an eternity.

I never did like people staring at me. Just last week in Walmart I got so mad I almost pissed my pants 'cause people were staring at me. A security guard stopped me and one of my little girls and wanted to search us. We hadn't stolen anything but my skin is dark enough to make security guards think I probably have. Skin color really puts you in the limelight in this area.

For instance, some of the kids at my daughter's school won't play with her. "My mama says I can't hold hands with you 'cause you're not like us," one of the little prissy bitches told her. And my son keeps getting pulled over by white cops. His skin is just dark enough to make them suspicious. Ain't life fun for Indians in the suburbs?

Damn, sometimes I hate being Indian. Ain't no way I can get out of it, though. Not like old Sergeant Sims here. I can't be Indian when convenient.

Nosirree. Not me. Not in the cards. Damn these cuffs are hurting my wrists. I wish I could have a smoke.

"Hey, Sara, stop blubbering and get me a cigarette."

"Where are the kids?" she asks as she lights my cigarette with shaking hands.

"I took them over to mama's last night." Damn this smoke tastes good.

"You put that knife right in his heart," Sara whispers so loud everyone in the room can hear. I look over to the body and realize she is right.

"He shouldn't have done what he did, Sara. He shouldn't have done what he did."

"What did he do, Mam?" Who is this man talking to me? He ain't a cop. If he is, he ain't wearing a uniform. Oh, he must be a detective, or something. I'm going to ignore him 'cause I don't like the way he smells. I swear some people think you can cover up an ugly face with sweet smelling cologne.

Damn, what was that? Moaning? He's alive! The sumbitch is alive! I guess I didn't stick that knife in far enough. Or maybe the heart I was aiming for is all dried up. Just dried up from having no feelings inside. Look at all those medical people hovering over him like he was some kind of prize or something. I bet if he was laying out on the street like that, bleeding and all, they wouldn't stop to give him the time of day.

"Mam, we're going to take you in now for questioning." It's that sweet smelling suit guy again. I'm still going to ignore him. His smell reminds me too much of that security guard at Walmart last week.

OK, now. I have to get my mind straight. "Sara, you go over to mama's and bring the girls to your house, OK? Tell them I'll be over to get them soon enough."

My crazy, loud-mouth sister Reni comes running into the house, demanding to know what in the hell is going on. "Well, you finally lost it, didn't you? You finally lost it. What the hell did he do this time, Honey? Finally did something to push you over the edge, didn't he? What was it? Did you catch him cheating again? Did he steal money from your purse again? Hit one of the kids? What was it?"

I look around at the mess in my house. Blood is everywhere. My husband is moaning and saying "Bitch" over and over. About twenty eyes are staring at me, waiting for an answer. I say loud enough for everyone to hear, "He kicked my dog. He kicked my dog and said it was too Indian to live here."

I walk out of my house, cops holding my arms, and get into the back seat of the patrol car. "Hey, can I have another smoke?" I say to no one in particular.

Sergeant Sims, AKA Indian When Convenient, lights a Marlboro Light and puts it between my lips. Looking out the back window of the patrol car, I see dark clouds rolling up over my house. Looks like it's going to rain. Again.

At least this ain't being filmed for one of those cop shows on TV, I think as we head downtown. Ah, the life of the gifted!

RUMORS

RUMORS

It was rumored that Addy May Birdsong would sneak into your house, touch your forehead with her fingers while you were sleeping, and change the course of your dreams. I had heard this rumor for the first time when I was about thirteen. Lydia Rattler, who sat next to me in Home Room, told me this because she had heard that Addy May was related to me.

"So what?" I had said back to her. "Everybody's related to everybody here." I had never liked Lydia much because she had ugly teeth that stuck way out and because she wanted to gossip all the time like an old woman. But she sat next to me that whole school year and I learned to endure her gossip, if not her buck teeth.

When I had asked my mama about the rumor, she said that lots of things were said about Addy May because she was different than most.

"What do you mean, different?" I asked in total sincerity. It seemed to me that almost every adult I knew back then had some sort of strangeness about them – mostly caused from alcohol, or from running out of it.

"Well," my mama had said thoughtfully as she scratched her chin the way she often did when she was trying to explain something in terms that she thought I might understand, "Cousin Addy May just has a way of stirring up people. She looks all the way into their souls with those black–pitted eyes of hers and it makes people wonder if she knows what they've been up to." I had to agree with the part about the black-pitted eyes. They reminded me of a tunnel a train had just gone through.

"But you don't pay any mind to what you hear about her. She's your cousin and she's had a hard life, harder than most on this reservation, and so she deserves to be a little stranger than most if she wants."

I forgot about my "stranger than most" Cousin Addy May and all the rumors about her until one night it was so hot I was having trouble sleeping and decided to crawl out the bedroom window to get some fresh air. I was careful not to wake my younger twin sisters. Course I loved them with all my heart, but they could be quite bothersome when I wanted some time alone.

The night air was so cool and refreshing I pulled my braids on top of my head and let it touch the back of my neck. It made me feel really good, so I decided to take a walk down the road that led up the mountain to our house. The two other families who lived on the road were at least two miles away, so I felt like I had the road all to myself. I had walked for about ten minutes, staring up at the stars and the full moon, feeling proud that I was so brave to be out by myself that late at night, when I saw Addy May standing there in the middle of the road with the moon shining down on her head like a flashlight. Her hair was long and loose, not braided as usual, and I remember thinking that it looked like a thick, black waterfall flowing down her skinny back. I was totally shocked to see someone standing there in the middle of the night and grateful that she hadn't heard me coming down the road.

She had her back to me, so I stepped into the darkness of the brush beside the road so I could watch her. She was wearing a long cotton skirt that was probably dark blue but looked purple in the moonlight, and a shawl of many colors was draped loosely around her thin shoulders. I watched quietly as she swayed her body back and forth, waving both hands above her head. The more I watched her, the faster my heart beat. And when she starting singing, I felt like it would bust right out of my chest. Her voice was beautiful, high pitched and full of rich guttural tones. Over and over she sang her song, swaying there in the moonlight. I could hear her words distinctly:

"First I was woman
then I was mother
now I am woman again."

Mesmerized by her presence and her voice, I had no idea what her song was about, but I knew the words came from way down deep inside her. From the same place my moon time had begun flowing several months back when mama had told me that I had become a woman. Addy May's words came from the connecting source to the earth that every woman has inside her, and my stomach burned way down deep in that spot as I listened.

I must have stood there in the brush for at least half an hour, watching her, listening to her singing, and feeling my heart trying to jump up into my throat. Then something happened that I never would have believed if someone else had told me about it. There were two female spirits come down from the sky and stood right next to Addy May's swaying body. One was real old and the other a young girl just a little older than me. With quick, jerky movements, they began to dance around Addy May, looking kind of like the white curling smoke that dances around a red hot fire, and chanting in Cherokee. I couldn't understand all of what they were saying because I don't speak my native language proper, but I heard a few words I could recognize and realized the gist of their song had to do with sorrow and grief.

As I stood there, squinting my eyes trying to figure out what was in the bundles each spirit woman carried in her arms, and muster up enough courage to stay and see what would happen next, Addy May turned and looked directly at me. I swear she looked directly at me and smiled right into my eyes, never missing a beat to her swaying or a word to her song. When she did that, I ran back home as fast as I could and didn't tell a soul what I had seen that night. Not even my mama. As a matter of fact, I kind of forgot about the incident for a while because my thoughts were on other things. Mostly my new boyfriend, Roger. That is until I heard from Lydia Rattler that Addy May had been arrested for stealing a baby boy.

She had gone into John and Amanda Wolfe's house late one night and taken their baby right from his crib. The baby hadn't cried or made any noise or anything, so the parents didn't know he was missing until his mama woke up the next morning and went to check on him. He was only six months old but he was big for his age. I had seen him in front of the Spirits on the River with his mama the week before Addy May stole him. Amanda had gone in there to apply for a job and asked me and my cousin Lenny, who happened to be walking by at the time, to hold him for her while she went in the restaurant to get an application. It was really curious to me that I had actually held that same baby in my arms just a week before Addy May stole him.

She hadn't tried to hide him or anything, and that's why they found out so quick that she had him. She had just taken him home with her, and when Mavis Rose had passed by Addy May's house on her way to the Tribal Offices as she did every weekday morning, she had seen Addy May sitting there on her front porch in an old rocking chair, holding him. Mavis said later that she thought it was kind of odd, Addy May sitting there on her front porch with a baby and all, but didn't know how odd until she arrived at work and was told that the Wolfe baby was missing. Of course she told all of them at the Tribal Offices what she had seen and they called the Wolfes who had Addy May arrested. The baby wasn't hurt or anything, so the Wolfe's didn't press it. The authorities let Addy May go after a good talking to because they didn't know what else to do with her, I guess.

Mama said she probably needed some kind of professional help 'cause she had never got over the death of her two babies who had burned to death that past winter. One was a girl, about a year-and-a-half-old, and the other a boy, six-months old. Her old mobile home had caught fire because of bad wiring or something, and she hadn't been able to save them.

I cried after my mama told me that story. I cried like I had never cried for anybody before because I felt close to Addy May somehow. So I went to visit her about a week after that. I just stopped by her house on my way home from school one day to tell her I was her cousin and just to see how she was doing. She didn't talk much, just nodded her head a little, and gave me some water from her well to drink. I can still taste that water now, all fresh and cool and sweet from that dipper gourd she used. I stayed for about an hour I guess, just sitting there on her front porch with her, not talking. And that was OK with me 'cause I felt like I just needed to be there for her. She never mentioned that night I had seen her in the road, swaying and singing, but I knew she knew. And I knew she knew that I cared about her.

I didn't go back to visit her again, but I did see her at different times, walking around, mumbling to herself. She got real crazy after the Wolfe baby incident and people just kind of left her alone and made up more rumors about her to entertain themselves. She wasn't a real threat to anybody, and the Crowe Sisters who lived down the road from her always made sure she had something to eat.

I guess I just grew up and forgot about her for several years. There were my two kids and a husband to worry over, and I hadn't thought about her for a while until Mama told me that Addy May had died. She had gotten the flu or pneumonia or something, and passed to spirit in her sleep one night.

"She's probably better off," Mama had said. I quietly agreed 'cause deep inside I knew that Addy May was with those two spirits who understood the song she was singing that night there in the middle of the road. The night she was swaying and singing in the moonlight, and I stood in the darkness of the brush, quietly watching and listening.

THE COLORED MOUNTAIN

THE COLORED MOUNTAIN

"It's raining colors," Anna says aloud, although there is no one to hear. The early morning rain has given the leaves just the encouragement they need to let go and begin falling, circling invisible foes and dancing with one another as they make the journey to their chosen resting place. "Yes, it's autumn time again," she smiles, revealing many missing teeth. "Time to go over there behind that colored mountain and rake off that place."

After a meal of sassafras tea and dried apples, she wraps an old multicolored knitted shawl about her aging shoulders, adjusts the bright red scarf around her silver hair, and begins to make her way down the path leading from her cabin. She uses a hand-carved hickory walking stick to balance her feeble body as her right leg drags noticeably, leaving strange marks in the dirt. Out of habit, she turns slightly to see if her old shaggy dog Wa'ya is following. It is a full moment before she realizes he has died the winter before. "Of course," she reminds herself, "he will be waiting for me when I get there."

It has been a long while since Anna has been to that place. The last time her granddaughters came to visit, they strictly forbade her to go back there this year. They said it was too long a walk for an old woman, and promised that when the leaves began to fall, they would go and clean it for her. Of course, she knew they wouldn't. They had too many important things to take care of, like making sure their daughters entered the Miss Fall Festival Contest, and making sure their husbands had been spending their time where they said they had. "Oh well, they will soon learn," she chuckles to the crows flying overhead.

A strong wind, gusting from the ridge behind her, almost knocks her to the ground. Her old tattered shawl falls from around her shoulders down to her thick waist, but she doesn't notice. She has something of much importance on her mind. After walking for almost twenty minutes on the rocky path through the forest, she stops by a swollen creek to rest for a spell. Taking the small cloth bag which she keeps pinned underneath her dress, she pulls open the tie strings and takes two pinches of tobacco. One she tosses to the swift, talking water, and one she slips inside her cheek. Such good sweet, Indian tobacco, grown in her own backyard, refreshes her soul as well as her mouth.

As Anna looks into the water, she begins to think of her husband. He has been gone to Spirit for over ten years now, and still she misses him. As she again begins to walk, she allows thoughts to fill her mind to take the pain away from her tired legs as she climbs the steep mountain path. But the bad memories try to overtake her. The memories of the alcohol and what it did to her husband. How it could turn him from a sweet and gentle man into a raging fool, striking at her and the children.

No one could understand why Anna just didn't leave him – go back to her mama's place in Soco and leave him be with his drunken friends. But she couldn't leave him, she loved him. She loved the way he always looked so handsome when his hair was freshly braided. She loved the shine that came to his dark eyes all the six times she had told him she was pregnant. No, she couldn't leave him, so she always forgave him. She knew it wasn't him that did those bad things: – it was the alcohol.

"I'm coming, U dv sa nv hi," she spoke softly under her breath, knowing he could hear her. She supposed he heard everything he wanted to now and was able to know all the time what was going on with the family he had left behind. Did he remember, as she did, the times the great grandchildren would come to visit and sit in their laps and ask for stories to be told? Did he know they never visited now that they were teenagers and had so many more important things to do other than visit their U ni li si?

Did he think about the two children they had lost: the eldest son and the middle daughter? After the car wreck that took both their lives, he had stopped drinking. He didn't touch a drink for the last twelve years of his life, once he found out that his son was just doing what he had seen his papa do – get drunk to forget his troubles.

Anna had been in the back yard working on her herb garden, when they had come to tell her two of her children had been killed down on Highway 19, just a few miles west of Bryson City. Why had they gone out and gotten so drunk and then tried to drive back home early that morning? She had wondered this so many times. Anna would never understand the actions of those who drank so heavily, but she had learned to forgive.

The sun was shining through the leaves in the forest now, forming a splotched pattern on the shawl dragging behind her in the dirt. Anna stopped suddenly as the place came into view. There it was, in the grove of hemlock trees just as she had remembered. She put her walking stick down beside her and begin to clear the dead leaves from the tops of the graves. Only two had distinct markers: large rocks with the names of her children carved on them. She had never allowed anyone to mark the grave of her husband. "I'll always know where I put him," she would tell them. "I don't need a marker to show me."

As she pulled the last of the leaves from the flat ground, she noticed a tiny rock next to the grave of her husband. "Oh, Wa'ya, I almost forgot you. Course, I knew you would be here to greet me."

She lay down in a little clearing not far from the place, spreading her shawl beneath her aching body. "Time for A ga yv li ge i to take a nap."

As her body began to breathe the deep breaths of sleep, she began to dream. And she dreamed the colored mountain was covered with red and green apples, bright, bright oranges, yellow ripe bananas, and soft purple grapes. It was as though the Creator had taken huge wagon loads of newly ripened fruit and emptied them down into the lush green valleys for all creatures to enjoy. Walking down the colored mountain was her husband carrying a basket of fresh beautiful fruit.

"It's really good to see you, Anna," he said as he handed her the basket. She saw he also had a handful of wild flowers picked especially for her. Smiling at him, she turned and looked behind her, but there was nothing there. Taking one last deep breath, her body relaxed. Anna knew she was going to sleep for a long, long time.

notes:
U dv sa nv hi: Old man
A ga yv li ge i: Old woman
Wa'ya: Wolf

HOWANETTA AND THE EYES OF THE DEAD

MariJo Moore

HOWANETTA AND THE EYES OF THE DEAD

There are some who are never able to leave the shadow of responsibility. They live on an oasis of "what was," in a desert of "what will be," in a world of "what is." I, Howanetta, am one of these people. I was born looking into the world of the dead. I can see, speak with, and feel them all the time. As a strong woman of medicine, perhaps I would have been better off being born a hundred years ago.

Soul dust began gathering on my eyelids at the age of six months. The soul dust of my grandmothers who had gone before. By the time I was sixteen, I could see as they see – with no restrictions. I could see clearly through the eyes of the dead.

People thought I was tormented by devils, strange in the head, somewhat provocative. My mother protected me from those who made fun of me, hid me from those who could not accept my difference, and pulled me from the grips of those who tried to flaunt me.

As I grew older, I saw things others refused to believe could exist. Through the eyes of the dead I saw the place where hummingbirds and cacti hold tiny hands and speak of their similarities. The place where white owls roost with brown sparrows and remember what was. Where red foxes sleep next to black bears and discuss what will be. Where yellow poppies grow in white snow and share knowledge of what is. Where everything is interlaced with a seed of something else and grows to fruition through the realization all is a part of the whole.

Taking long night walks through the memories of the dead ones, I rarely saw things I did not want to see. My favorite times

72

were watching the tinkling of tiny copper bells strapped to the ankles, wrists and breasts of the dead ones. Bells which echoed their laughter that was not unlike the tinkling of the tiny copper bells.

Looking into the landscape of the moon – the ever present, ever giving moon – I saw the dead ones dancing, their movements causing the waters of rivers to shake and rumble and smile. I often saw myself as the dead ones saw me looking at them looking back at me.

All was so exciting and entertaining, so utterly inviting that I refrained from discovering or realizing a different existence for a very long time.

But eventually, I grew lonely for humans. I married a man who would never believe me and raised four children who were afraid of me. The husband left and the children grew to find lives of their own. Then I knew it was time to look again through the eyes of the dead.

After seven long night walks of seven years each, filled with tinkling tiny copper bells, and the dance of shaking, rumbling, smiling waters, I was ready for the change. Looking though the eyes of the dead had been delightful, yes, entertaining, yes, unavoidable, absolutely, but the time had come to become even more responsible.

Taking a long silken feather from an arrangement left in the corner of my mind by a beautiful male peacock, I lightly brushed away the soul dust that had gathered on my eyelids through the years. This feather full of soul dust I placed ever so gently (carefully avoiding the breezes that swept in from the dancing, rumbling, smiling river waters) inside a beaded box shining sweetly. I closed the lid securely and left the soul dust there, safe from harm's way. Having seen mostly good through the eyes of the dead, I readied myself for a new vision.

I fasted and prayed and sang and fasted and prayed and sang until I was prepared for the new vision. What I saw disturbed me greatly. A Spirit Woman in the guise of my second greatest grandmother came to visit. Looking though her eyes, I saw the vision she had been given not so long ago.

I shared this vision with many, hoping to find others who could see through the eyes of the dead. Hoping they would take heed, listen, even reveal they had been shown the same vision.

I am still waiting, even though it has been years since I first shared the vision. My determination has not changed. I wait and wait for others to come to their sixth senses, hoping it will never become too late.

This is the vision I share:

I stared at the mountain until I began to see it breathe. Until it was no longer a single, solitary rock, but a living part of the whole. It became the arms of trees reaching up to touch the sky, the breast of the river swelling outside itself, the mirror of all things past and all things present. It became more than a mountain. It became everything.

A strong breeze lapped at my face. Hard rain spat in my eyes. I could hear the heart of the Earth hammering beneath my feet and feel the beatings all the way to my knees. I knew the sun had begun its daily bleeding into the valleys behind me but I could not turn around. I stood there and stared straight ahead until there was nothing left to see. Until night swallowed all things past and all things present. Until it swallowed everything. But still I couldn't cry.

The pain was so deep I couldn't touch it to name it or find it with my imagination. So deep I couldn't reach inside and pull it out or push inside to make it go deeper. It was real. So real I could feel it choking itself on my innards. And so I waited, there in the wet dark, until it had its fill of me. Until everything inside of me began to move.

All my memories began to remember themselves and all my dreams began to redream themselves. My heart hurt. My head hurt. All of my body ached and my eyes burned. Not because of what they saw but because of what they were to see. And still I couldn't cry.

I continued to pray into the night and all through the next day. I knew I would have died there that second night had the vision not come.

The dark solidness opened before me as I watched the workings of Spirit manifesting before me, gifting me with the answer to what seemed like month-long prayers. Sweat beaded on my forehead. I smelled my own fear, tasted it as the beads ran down my lips. What I saw frightened but did not surprise me.

Mighty mountains crumbled, strong rivers flowed backwards, and age old trees uprooted themselves. People of all colors ran, screamed, begged for mercy. But Earth had had enough abuse, enough neglect. Earth was shedding Herself of those who had no respect for Her gifts and bounties. As an irritated dog shakes fleas from its body, Earth shook the humans who irritated Her.

And then the air was still. Black and solid. The night closed around me as quickly as it had opened. As I fell to my knees, I knew what I had seen was to happen if changes were not made. If hearts were not cleansed of hatred and judgment, if respect was not remembered, if the old ways of honor were not restored, my vision would become a reality. Earth could and would reject us. For Earth is wise and knows that we need Her much more than She needs us.

The creeping dawn found my eyes full of water. As I lay face down, my tears melting into the vastness beneath my tired body, I could hear the all-knowing winds whispering over and over:

"What is not loved and respected will be taken away. What humans attempt to control, eventually controls them."

THE TASTE OF INSANITY

THE TASTE OF INSANITY

(This story in my belly has got to come out. It's got to come out or I believe I am gonna bust open just like an overripe watermelon laying right out there in the field, sleeping in the hot sunlight.)

Ada

"You can't take other people's problems too personally," Mama said, wiping bacon grease from her fingers onto her worn-out apron. The apron was so old and faded you couldn't even tell what the print was, just that there was once something drawn on the fabric. I think it may have been tiny blue birds. She was cooking breakfast for us children that Sunday morning just like she did every Sunday morning, right before sending us to church. She'd been making biscuits and I couldn't tell if all the gray in her hair was there naturally or maybe just little bits of flour she had brushed into it as she wiped her forehead. It could get awfully hot in that kitchen, cooking with that wood–burning stove.

"What do you mean, I can't take other people's problems too personally?" I'm eleven and suppose to help Mama cook, but mostly I just sit around watching her. You can learn quite a bit watching other people cook – especially my mama because she is gifted in the ways of preparing food.

"Well, if you think too much about other people's doings, it might just make you worry too much and too much worry can make you sick," Mama said. My stomach froze because my mama was one of the worst worriers I had ever known. She had lines in her forehead that looked like you could plant a row of potatoes in.

And they were all from worrying.

"You just can't be responsible for other people's ways," she said. You can't make them change, and you can't make them do what you think they ought to do no matter how hard you try. And you can't help one soul on God's green earth if they don't want help." Mama had begun saying things like "God's green earth" ever since she started going to church. She's Indian, same as her mama was and she never went to church, but my mama had decided it was the thing to do after some ladies from a church not too far from our home started coming around and spreading what they called the gospel. This was about the same time Papa took to staying out all night, drinking and carousing around. Now Mama goes to church every Sunday, rain or shine, and makes all us go, too. Except for Talalah, who's the oldest. Mama can't get her to do much of nothing since she met Colt.

"But Mama, he's mean to Talalah. I know he is because I've heard them fighting, and there she is spending all her time with him! He's mean to her, Mama. I hear tell that he leaves her sitting outside in his ragged old car while he goes inside that pool room over in Chattanooga for hours at a time."

"I reckon that's her business if she wants to sit there and wait on him."

"Well, he must have something pretty special is all I can say."

Mama ignored this remark and I was kinda glad. I didn't want another lecture on sex. Not anytime soon.

After a few minutes of silence, watching Mama crack egg shell after egg shell and pour the insides into a hot greased skillet, I said with all the courage I could muster, "I think he's just too much like Papa."

When she heard that, my mama laid down what she was doing, pulled off her apron, threw it on the back of one of the skinny kitchen chairs, and walked quietly out of the room. I knew

I had gone too far and would be in charge of making sure all the other children got their breakfast. Sometimes I'm bad about letting my mouth overload my butt.

Talalah

Last Thursday. That was the day it began. The day before it had rained all day and into the deepest part of the night. I didn't get much rest that night which was odd because pouring rain always opens a doorway to comforting sleep for me. Instead I tossed and turned, turned and tossed, wrapped up in sweaty dreams.

Then around dawn I tasted it for the first time. On my tongue at first, then my throat. It was as if someone had slipped the taste into my mouth without my knowing what was happening. But deep within, I really wasn't surprised. I had known it was coming.

It was like the smell of rust. My first taste of insanity. Bitter but not totally unpleasant. And it hurt. I swallowed hard several times to make it go away but it remained just under my tongue, lining the left side of my throat, scratching at my thoughts like a spoiled kitten demanding attention. I spoke to no one about it. Tried to ignore the taste until finally, sometime late that night, it left. But I know it'll be back. Just like I knew it was coming. I'd seen the signs of it for about two weeks. That was about the time I started drinking again.

For over four months, I didn't touch alcohol. Turned down every opportunity (and there were plenty) to drown my sorrows in that evil liquid. To search for escape in its subtle calling. My last drunk, up until two weeks ago, had been on my wedding night. Me and my new husband, Colt, had both gotten "rip–roaring," as he liked to call it, and fell asleep in each other's arms, too exhausted and drunk to make love. Before morning he got up, went into the little bathroom of our honeymoon cabin, and shot himself through the mouth with a gun he had borrowed from a friend just before the wedding. He left me a note on the tiny oak nightstand, right next to our marriage license.

Dear Talalah,
I just can't seem to figure out my purpose here in this life so I'm going to Spirit to try and make a go of it there. Loved you till the day I died.

Tsa Yo Ga

He signed it with his Cherokee name. I think it is such a beautiful name. I still keep the note pinned just inside my bra, folded neatly inside a little bitty piece of aluminum foil. I took it out and looked at it last Thursday for the first time in several weeks. The ink was beginning to fade where the creases had cut into his last written words, but I know them by heart anyway. His Cherokee name, scrawled across the bottom as if it were a small baby bird scurrying to get off the paper, leaped up at me like it always does when I look at the note.

I remember the day he asked me to marry him. We were lying on his mama's red wool blanket along the banks of the Hiwassee River. He was drinking beer after beer and began to tell about his daddy. I had heard rumors about this man before, but I never would have associated him with the young man I had fallen for. I never would have dreamed this white man would have anything to do with an Indian woman, much less father an Indian baby. And even though Colt didn't tell me whether or not he had ever spent time with his daddy, I knew he hadn't. I just knew it.

Then Colt told me about his Indian name. About how his Grandmama Twister had given it to him, and how proud he was of it. But I could tell he didn't feel like he deserved it. I imagine that is because he was part white. I really don't know. He choked on the name at first, then took a deep breath and said it proudly. Then he screamed it into the heart of a nearby mountain and struggled to his feet to try and catch the echo coming back to him. When I asked him about this name after he had sobered up the next day, he acted as though I had asked him to expose his privates in public. I didn't mention it again. But now I have it, in his own handwriting, to carry with me forever, close to my heart, close to where he loved to lay his head.

****

(I guess it was the spirit of the thing that got to me. The spirit of suicide. Sure, I felt sorry for Talalah, losing her new husband like that just after her wedding and all. But deep inside it was the spirit of the suicide that got to me. Kinda like it came to live with me - to pester me. Because it's like this: I knew this was going to happen all along. I knew it, I don't know how I knew it but I just knew it. I mean, it was a bad dream, but I kept dreaming it anyway. I had the sign that something bad was going to happen. Maybe I shoulda done something. But what?)

****

Ada

I heard the yelling in the front room. It woke me up and I crawled out of bed and sneaked around behind the couch to see what was going on. It was Talalah and Mama.

"That boy ain't nothing but trouble, Talalah. He ain't going to bring this family nothing but shame."

"This family shame? Hah! I don't want to hear nothing else

about him because I love him and that's all there is to it. Papa said I could marry him and I'm gonna."

"That drunken fool will do nothing but lead you straight to the ever-lasting fires of hell."

"Now who ever heard of a true Indian believing in such a place? What's got into you?"

At that point I sneezed because there was so much dust behind the couch and they both hushed.

Colt

Hey, Mama. It's me. Your son, Colt. I got to tell you some things, Mama. Got to clear some things up so my spirit can rest. It was that Tuesday in April when the sun looked like the moon all day. Talalah and I were out walking, not going anywhere in particular, just walking along in this great big meadow over by the Hiwassee River. There were no trees in that meadow. I remember that for sure. It looked like something big, really big, had stomped all the trees down into the ground so all that was left were these little scraggly kind of bushes. Anyways we had walked for about ten or fifteen minutes through that treeless meadow when all of a sudden Talalah hollered out, "Look at that!" And there, just underneath my left foot was a blue jay. It wasn't dead, but pretty close to it, so I picked it up to see if there was anything I could do to help it.

Mama, it had a cracked beak. It was cracked right in two along the top part. I held that bird in my hand, and while I was looking at its cracked beak, it died. Right there in my hand and that's when I knew that it was time for me to take the plunge. Into darkness. Into the other realm because I knew it was a sign, and, Mama, it was just my time to go.

So I asked Talalah to marry me and even though I had only known her for a short while, I felt like I had always known her. I couldn't barely stand the thought of leaving her, but I wanted to make damn sure that she would grieve me after I took the plunge into the other realm. So I asked her to marry me, and she did and that night I shot myself.

Mama, I know all of this is just coming to you in a dream so please try to pay attention because I want you to know that I love you with all my heart and that I wouldn't have done a thing to cause you any pain but it was just my time.

I know I drank a lot. Drank a lot more than I should have, but, Mama, sometimes that question inside of me of why I was born part Indian and part white would come up and make my throat so dry, scratch all the wetness from it. I just had to take a quick drink to soothe it. To push that question back down inside my guts, I had to keep on taking quick drinks, and before I would know it, I'd be drunk. Rip-roaring drunk.

I'm sorry, Mama. I love you with all my heart. I know you always told me that alcohol would destroy me, but I guess I was secretly hoping it would destroy the baddest part of me. The mean part where all those thoughts of trying to fit in came from. I'm sorry, Mama. I loved you with all my heart and I know it wasn't your intention to cause this question to explode inside of me when you gave me life. I know you didn't do all the choosing. It was him that chose to ignore me. To pretend I didn't exist. I just couldn't ever really figure out why, Mama. Why?

Silence.

I know something now, Mama. I know that the answer was close to me. It was so close it was lying between my eyelashes. So close it was in the spit in my mouth. So close, Mama, so close I couldn't find it. So close it was in my skin. It was in my skin, Mama. It was in my skin.

Don't cry no more.

Sing for me, Mama. Sing for me. Sing one of them pretty gospels in Cherokee. Sing *Amazing Grace*. You know, the one they sang on the Trail of Tears? Ain't no end to that trail, is there, Mama? Sing for me, Mama, sing for me, sweet and soft-like like you used to ....

> *Oo ne hla nuh hi, oo we ji*
> *i ga goo yuh hi i*
> *hna gwo jo suh wi oo lo se*
> *i ga goo yuh ho nuh.*

S gi, Mama. That's it. Thank you.

Talalah

It took me a while to pull myself together and find some semblance of sense to life after Colt's death. I felt like I had always been with him, even though I had known him only six or seven weeks when he proposed that day down by the river. He had found a dead bird and it had upset him but he didn't talk about it. Now that I think of it, it was a dead blue jay. Maybe it meant something to him since his Cherokee name means blue jay and all, I don't know, but he asked me to marry him.

"Why not? he asked me. "We love each other and we need to be together." His dark eyes had shone like cloudy pearls and I had agreed, "Why not, indeed!"

That very same week I wore my favorite beaded white cotton dress and married him. I never felt more beautiful or more alive. Three days later, I wore the same dress to my young husband's funeral. And even today, a week after tasting my insanity for the first time, I still feel as if a part of me was buried with him that Spring day four months ago.

Ada

After Colt killed himself, I got to wondering pretty hard about the ever lasting fires of hell Mama was always talking about. Is there such a place down below the earth? I didn't know exactly how I could find out, but it kept me awake for about three nights, and when I heard my Grandpa Jumper was coming to visit us, I figured he'd know. He's about sixty and I guess he must know everything there is to know about this world and what's below it.

The best explanation I had been able to come up with on my own was that all that could possibly be beneath the earth is what's above it. Sky and stars and such. I mean, if the world really is round like that globe I saw in Mrs. Hudson's Science class, then what could be underneath the earth except what's above it ? And how could there be fires that never went out? I told Grandpa Jumper all this when I asked him and he was quiet for a long time. Thinking I guess. He's a most quite man and a deep, deep thinker. I guess that's why I like him so much. He reminds me a little of how I would like to be if I could keep my mouth shut more.

He looked deep into my eyes, trying to figure where I had come up with this question I guess, and then after what seemed like the length of two long recesses back to back, he spoke. Soft and calm like, using the same tone he would have used if I had asked him what time of day it was.

"I reckon I ain't never seen a fire that didn't sooner or later burn itself out."

That was all he said on the matter and that answer settled it for me. I slept real good that night. But that was before Colt shot himself.

Talalah

I found him, you know. There on that tiny, cold bathroom floor. I can't describe to you what a mess it was and I can't really explain why I didn't hear the gun shot unless, of course, it was because I was so passed out from the whiskey. But when I saw him laying there, all beautiful and ugly at the same time, there was something that came from deep in my guts and it wanted out bad, so bad it was scratching at my throat but I couldn't let it out. I couldn't because I guess I just went apeshit, seeing him there like that and all. I couldn't let anything like what was clawing at my innards come out of my mouth. Not then. Not there.

But last Thursday it finally made its way up into my mouth and I tasted it. I tasted the insanity. I guess I'd held it back a long time and when my body began to lose itself to the whiskey, it got just too weak to hold it down there in my guts any longer.

And now I taste it and now it is thick and I can see it on the end of my tongue and I can hear a blue jay squawking outside my rainy window and I know…I know.

****

(So now I've got this story out of me and I feel better and now my guts won't try to bust open like an overripe watermelon lying out there in the field, sleeping in the hot sunlight. Now maybe I can get some rest and my belly will stop jumping up and down with nervousness. I knew it, you know. I knew he was going to kill himself. I don't know how I knew, but I knew. It was a bad dream, but I kept on dreaming it anyway, and then it happened and now I've told it and here it is. Now I can go on with this business of becoming a spirit to watch over my family. I've told the truth. I knew that boy was going to kill himself. I knew, but I didn't know what to do to stop him. Thanks for listening to this story. It helps me feel better having it outside my belly. I don't feel so swollen now. Now, I can go on.)

SUDA CORNSILK'S GATHERING

SUDA CORNSILK'S GATHERING

Suda Cornsilk sat for a long time around the storyteller's ceremonial fire, listening and gathering. Listening to learn, gathering to remember. Close to the center of the night she returned home, and began to comb from her long, thick hair the words of the tribal stories she had gathered.

Suda watched as the words fell, releasing themselves from their nestled resting places. Watched as the age-old words hit the earth, bounced lightly, then settled into a pile of colorful dances. Purple circling words of laughter, silver floating words of wisdom, green twirling words of healing, blue floating words of gratitude, and yellow stomping words of hope. Necessary and magnificent all.

Combing her dark smooth hair softly so as not to cause any erasure of the remaining words, Suda watched them falling, one by one, then two by two, quietly bumping into one another. But something was not right! The words had no order! There could be no meanings to these stories for her! The revered words were too jumbled, too meshed, too together!

As she began to weep, Suda suddenly remembered something very important. She touched the tiny braid of hair near her left ear. The tiny braid her mother had woven into her hair just a few days before. It is here she will find what she needs. Here is where the heart of the tribal stories are hiding.

As Suda slowly and carefully unwound the braid, out, out, and down floated four red words as sacred and important as fire. Words that gave a deeper meaning to the purple, silver, green, blue and yellow words that circled and danced around her. Words that made the tribal stories real, made them whole. From the tiny braid in her hair the gifted red words *respect, share, remember* and *persevere* softly fell. Suda watched gratefully as these words carefully joined with the others, making colorful sense of all.

The tribal stories were then in order, complete within themselves. Suda scooped them up, word by word, and placed them inside her open heart. After performing a ceremony of gratitude to the Spirits of the stories, and offering a sweet prayer of gratitude to her mother, Suda allowed a deep sleep to visit her shining dark eyes, bringing a welcomed restful night.

And for a long time – because of this gift from her mother and all the mothers before – Suda carried the stories of her people within easy reach inside the protected sanctuary of her heart.

Then one day Suda braided these stories into the hair of her daughter. When it was time, Suda's daughter shared them with her children, who shared them with their children, and on and on, until the memories of the stories, breathing and growing in the lives of many, kept strong, even when they became mixed with the blood of other races.

Today, the stories Suda Cornsilk gathered so long ago bleed and mix and blend and renew and grow and sing and dance and weave themselves into the lives of all of Suda's descendants. These stories will continue multiplying, gathering new ways of survival to live inside the old ways of learning, as long as Indian blood runs through the veins of those who respect, share, remember and persevere. Which could be forever.

ABOUT THE AUTHOR

MariJo Moore, of Cherokee, Irish and Dutch ancestry is an author/artist/poet/journalist. She was chosen as one of the top five American Indian writers of the new century by *Native Peoples* magazine (June/July 2000 issue). In 1998, she was honored with the prestigious award of North Carolina's Distinguished Woman of the Year in the Arts. Her works have appeared in numerous magazines, newspapers, anthologies and journals. She serves on the board of the North Carolina Humanities Council and the National Caucus of Wordcraft Circle of Native Writers. She resides in the mountains of Western North Carolina and travels widely to present lectures/literary readings and creative writing workshops.

Website: marijomoore.com

ORDERING INFORMATION

books by MariJo Moore

Red Woman With Backward Eyes and Other Stories $16.00
Spirit Voices of Bones $16.00
Crow Quotes $8.00
Tree Quotes $8.00
Desert Quotes $8.00
Feeding The Ancient Fires: A Collection of Writings
by NC American Indians (editor) $15.00

All prices include shipping and handling. Send check or money order to:

rENEGADE pLANETS pUBLISHING
PO Box 2493
Candler, NC 28715

Thank you for supporting an American Indian owned company